Missing Link
&
Operation Haystack

Missing Link
&
Operation Haystack

Two Classic Stories by
FRANK HERBERT

PHOENIX PICK

an imprint of

ARC
MANOR
Rockville, Maryland

Missing Link was originally published as a story in *Astounding Science Fiction*, February 1959. *Operation Haystack* was originally published as a story in *Astounding Science Fiction, May* 1959.

ISBN: 978-1-60450-230-5

Visit
www.PhoenixPick.com
for more great sci-fi and fantasy

Published by Phoenix Pick
an imprint of Arc Manor
P. O. Box 10339
Rockville, MD 20849-0339
www.ArcManor.com

Printed in the United States of America / United Kingdom

CONTENTS

Missing Link

The Romantics used to say that the eyes were the windows of the Soul. A good Alien Xenologist might not put it quite so poetically...but he can, if he's sharp, read a lot in the look of an eye!

"WE OUGHT TO SCRAPE this planet clean of every living thing on it," muttered Umbo Stetson, section chief of Investigation & Adjustment.

Stetson paced the landing control bridge of his scout cruiser. His footsteps grated on a floor that was the rear wall of the bridge during flight. But now the ship rested on its tail fins—all four hundred glistening red and black meters of it. The open ports of the bridge looked out on the jungle roof of Gienah III some one hundred fifty meters below. A butter yellow sun hung above the horizon, perhaps an hour from setting.

"Clean as an egg!" he barked. He paused in his round of the bridge, glared out the starboard port, spat into the fire-blackened circle that the cruiser's jets had burned from the jungle.

The I-A section chief was dark-haired, gangling, with large head and big features. He stood in his customary slouch, a stance not improved by sack-like patched blue fatigues. Although on this present operation he rated the flag of a division admiral, his fatigues carried no insignia. There was a general unkempt, straggling look about him.

Lewis Orne, junior I-A field man with a maiden diploma, stood at the opposite port, studying the jungle horizon. Now and then he glanced at the bridge control console, the chronometer above it, the big translite map of their position tilted from the opposite bulkhead. A heavy planet native, he felt vaguely uneasy on this Gienah III with its gravity of only seven-eighths Terran Standard. The surgical scars on his neck where the micro-communications equipment had been inserted itched maddeningly. He scratched.

"Hah!" said Stetson. "Politicians!"

A thin black insect with shell-like wings flew in Orne's port, settled in his close-cropped red hair. Orne pulled the insect gently from his hair, released it. Again it tried to land in his hair. He ducked. It flew across the bridge, out the port beside Stetson.

There was a thick-muscled, no-fat look to Orne, but something about his blocky, off-center features suggested a clown.

"I'm getting tired of waiting," he said.

"*You're* tired! Hah!"

10

A breeze rippled the tops of the green ocean below them. Here and there, red and purple flowers jutted from the verdure, bending and nodding like an attentive audience.

"Just look at that blasted jungle!" barked Stetson. "Them and their stupid orders!"

A call bell tinkled on the bridge control console. The red light above the speaker grid began blinking. Stetson shot an angry glance at it. "Yeah, Hal?"

"O.K., Stet. Orders just came through. We use Plan C. ComGO says to brief the field man, and jet out of here."

"Did you ask them about using another field man?"

Orne looked up attentively.

The speaker said: "Yes. They said we have to use Orne because of the records on the *Delphinus*."

"Well then, will they give us more time to brief him?"

"Negative. It's crash priority. ComGO expects to blast the planet anyway."

Stetson glared at the grid. "Those fat-headed, lard-bottomed, pig-brained...POLITICIANS!" He took two deep breaths, subsided. "O.K. Tell them we'll comply."

"One more thing, Stet."

"What now?"

"I've got a confirmed contact."

Instantly, Stetson was poised on the balls of his feet, alert. "Where?"

"About ten kilometers out. Section AAB-6."

"How many?"

"A mob. You want I should count them?"

"No. What're they doing?"

"Making a beeline for us. You better get a move on."

"O.K. Keep us posted."

"Right."

Stetson looked across at his junior field man. "Orne, if you decide you want out of this assignment, you just say the word. I'll back you to the hilt."

"Why should I want out of my first field assignment?"

"Listen, and find out." Stetson crossed to a tilt-locker behind the big translite map, hauled out a white coverall uniform with gold insignia, tossed it to Orne. "Get into these while I brief you on the map."

"But this is an R&R uni—" began Orne.

"Get that uniform on your ugly frame!"

"Yes, sir, Admiral Stetson, sir. Right away, sir. But I thought I was through with old Rediscovery & Re-education when you drafted me off of Hamal into the I-A...sir." He began changing from the I-A blue to the R&R white. Almost as an afterthought, he said: "...Sir."

A wolfish grin cracked Stetson's big features. "I'm soooooo happy you have the proper attitude of subservience toward authority."

Orne zipped up the coverall uniform. "Oh, yes, sir... sir."

"O.K., Orne, pay attention." Stetson gestured at the map with its green superimposed grid squares. "Here we are. Here's that city we flew over on our way down. You'll head for it as soon as we drop you. The place is big enough that if you hold a course roughly northeast you can't miss it. We're—"

Again the call bell rang.

"What is it this time, Hal?" barked Stetson.

"They've changed to Plan H, Stet. New orders cut."

"Five days?"

"That's all they can give us. ComGO says he can't keep the information out of High Commissioner Bullone's hands any longer than that."

"It's five days for sure then."

"Is this the usual R&R foul-up?" asked Orne.

Stetson nodded. "Thanks to Bullone and company! We're just one jump ahead of catastrophe, but they still pump the bushwah into the Rah & Rah boys back at dear old Uni-Galacta!"

"You're making light of my revered alma mater," said Orne. He struck a pose. "We must reunite

13

the lost planets with our centers of culture and industry, and take up the glorious onward march of mankind that was so brutally—"

"Can it!" snapped Stetson. "We both know we're going to rediscover one planet too many some day. Rim War all over again. But this is a different breed of fish. It's not, repeat, *not* a *re*-discovery."

Orne sobered. "Alien?"

"Yes. A-L-I-E-N! A never-before-contacted culture. That language you were force fed on the way over, that's an alien language. It's not complete...all we have off the *minis*. And we excluded data on the natives because we've been hoping to dump this project and nobody the wiser."

"Holy mazoo!"

"Twenty-six days ago an I-A search ship came through here, had a routine mini-sneaker look at the place. When he combed in his net of sneakers to check the tapes and films, lo and behold, he had a little stranger."

"One of *theirs*?"

"No. It was a *mini* off the *Delphinus Rediscovery*. The *Delphinus* has been unreported for eighteen standard months!"

"Did it crack up here?"

"We don't know. If it did, we haven't been able to spot it. She was supposed to be way off in the Balandine System by now. But we've something else on our minds. It's the one item that makes me want to blot out this place, and run home with my tail between my legs. We've a—"

Again the call bell chimed.

"NOW WHAT?" roared Stetson into the speaker.

"I've got a *mini* over that mob, Stet. They're talking about us. It's a definite raiding party."

"What armament?"

"Too gloomy in that jungle to be sure. The infra beam's out on this *mini*. Looks like hard pellet rifles of some kind. Might even be off the *Delphinus*."

"Can't you get closer?"

"Wouldn't do any good. No light down there, and they're moving up fast."

"Keep an eye on them, but don't ignore the other sectors," said Stetson.

"You think I was born yesterday?" barked the voice from the grid. The contact broke off with an angry sound.

"One thing I like about the I-A," said Stetson. "It collects such even-tempered types." He looked at the white uniform on Orne, wiped a hand across his mouth as though he'd tasted something dirty.

"Why *am* I wearing this thing?" asked Orne.

"Disguise."

"But there's no mustache!"

Stetson smiled without humor. "That's one of I-A's answers to those fat-keistered politicians. We're setting up our own search system to find the planets before *they* do. We've managed to put spies in key places at R&R. Any touchy planets our spies report, we divert the files."

"Then what?"

"Then we look into them with bright boys like you—disguised as R&R field men."

"Goody, goody. And what happens if R&R stumbles onto me while I'm down there playing patty cake?"

"We disown you."

"But you said an I-A ship found this joint."

"It did. And then one of our spies in R&R intercepted a *routine* request for an agent-instructor to be assigned here with full equipment. Request signed by a First-Contact officer name of Diston...of the *Delphinus*!"

"But the Del—"

"Yeah. Missing. The request was a forgery. Now you see why I'm mostly for rubbing out this place. Who'd dare forge such a thing unless he knew for sure that the original FC officer was missing...or dead?"

"What the jumped up mazoo are we doing here, Stet?" asked Orne. "Alien calls for a full contact team with all of the—"

"It calls for one planet-buster bomb...buster—in five days. Unless you give them a white bill in the meantime. High Commissioner Bullone will have

word of this planet by then. If Gienah III still ex-
ists in five days, can't you imagine the fun the
politicians'll have with it? Mama mia! We want this
planet cleared for contact or dead before then."

"I don't like this, Stet."

"YOU don't like it!"

"Look," said Orne. "There must be another way.
Why...when we teamed up with the Alerinoids we
gained five hundred years in the physical sciences
alone, not to mention the—"

"The Alerinoids didn't knock over one of our survey
ships first."

"What if the *Delphinus* just crashed here...and the
locals picked up the pieces?"

"That's what you're going in to find out, Orne. But
answer me this: If they *do* have the *Delphinus*, how
long before a tool-using race could be a threat to
the galaxy?"

"I saw that city they built, Stet. They could be dug in
within six months, and there'd be no—"

"Yeah."

Orne shook his head. "But think of it: Two civilizations that matured along different lines! Think of
all the different ways we'd approach the same problems...the lever that'd give us for—"

"You sound like a Uni-Galacta lecture! Are you
through marching arm in arm into the misty
future?"

Orne took a deep breath. "Why's a freshman like me being tossed into this dish?"

"You'd still be on the *Delphinus* master lists as an R&R field man. That's important if you're masquerading."

"Am I the only one? I know I'm a recent *convert*, but—"

"You want out?"

"I didn't say that. I just want to know why I'm—"

"Because the bigdomes fed a set of requirements into one of their iron monsters. Your card popped out. They were looking for somebody capable, dependable...and...*expendable*!"

"Hey!"

"That's why I'm down here briefing you instead of sitting back on a flagship. *I* got you into the I-A. Now, you listen carefully: If you push the panic button on this one without cause, I will personally flay you alive. We both know the advantages of an alien contact. But if you get into a hot spot, and call for help, I'll dive this cruiser into that city to get you out!"

Orne swallowed. "Thanks, Stet. I'm—"

"We're going to take up a tight orbit. Out beyond us will be five transports full of I-A marines and a Class IX Monitor with one planet-buster. You're calling the shots, God help you! First, we want to know if they have the *Delphinus*...and if so, where it is. Next, we want to know just how warlike these goons are. Can we control them if they're bloodthirsty. What's their potential?"

"In five days?"

"Not a second more."

"What do we know about them?"

"Not much. They look something like an ancient Terran chimpanzee...only with blue fur. Face is hairless, pink-skinned." Stetson snapped a switch. The translite map became a screen with a figure frozen on it. "Like that. This is life size."

"Looks like the missing link they're always hunting for," said Orne. "Yeah, but you've got a different kind of a missing link."

"Vertical-slit pupils in their eyes," said Orne. He studied the figure. It had been caught from the front by a mini-sneaker camera. About five feet tall. The stance was slightly bent forward, long arms. Two vertical nose slits. A flat, lipless mouth. Receding chin. Four-fingered hands. It wore a wide belt from which dangled neat pouches and what looked like tools, although their use was obscure. There appeared to be the tip of a tail protruding from behind one of the squat legs. Behind the creature towered the faery spires of the city they'd observed from the air.

"Tails?" asked Orne.

"Yeah. They're arboreal. Not a road on the whole planet that we can find. But there are lots of vine

19

lanes through the jungles." Stetson's face hardened. "Match *that* with a city as advanced as that one."

"Slave culture?"

"Probably."

"How many cities have they?"

"We've found two. This one and another on the other side of the planet. But the other one's a ruin."

"A ruin? Why?"

"You tell us. Lots of mysteries here."

"What's the planet like?"

"Mostly jungle. There are polar oceans, lakes and rivers. One low mountain chain follows the equatorial belt about two thirds around the planet."

"But only two cities. Are you sure?"

"Reasonably so. It'd be pretty hard to miss something the size of that thing we flew over. It must be fifty kilometers long and at least ten wide. Swarming with these creatures, too. We've got a zone-count estimate that places the city's population at over thirty million."

"Whee-ew! Those are tall buildings, too."

"We don't know much about this place, Orne. And unless you bring them into the fold, there'll be nothing but ashes for our archaeologists to pick over."

"Seems a dirty shame."

"I agree, but—"

The call bell jangled.

Stetson's voice sounded tired: "Yeah, Hal?"

"That mob's only about five kilometers out, Stet. We've got Orne's gear outside in the disguised air sled."

"We'll be right down."

"Why a disguised sled?" asked Orne.

"If they think it's a ground buggy, they might get careless when you most need an advantage. We could always scoop you out of the air, you know."

"What're my chances on this one, Stet?"

Stetson shrugged. "I'm afraid they're slim. These goons probably have the *Delphinus*, and they want you just long enough to get your equipment and everything you know."

"Rough as that, eh?"

"According to our best guess. If you're not out in five days, we blast."

Orne cleared his throat.

"Want out?" asked Stetson.

"No."

"Use the *back-door* rule, son. Always leave yourself a way out. Now...let's check that equipment the surgeons put in your neck." Stetson put a hand to his throat. His mouth remained closed, but there was a surf-hissing voice in Orne's ears: "You read me?"

"Sure. I can—"

"No!" hissed the voice. "Touch the mike contact. Keep your mouth closed. Just use your speaking muscles without speaking."

Orne obeyed.

"O.K.," said Stetson. "You come in loud and clear."

"I ought to. I'm right on top of you!"

"There'll be a relay ship over you all the time," said Stetson. "Now...when you're not touching that mike contact this rig'll still feed us what you say... and everything that goes on around you, too. We'll monitor everything. Got that?"

"Yes."

Stetson held out his right hand. "Good luck. I meant that about diving in for you. Just say the word."

"I know the word, too," said Orne. "HELP!"

Gray mud floor and gloomy aisles between monstrous bluish tree trunks—that was the jungle. Only the barest weak glimmering of sunlight penetrated to the mud. The disguised sled—its para-grav units turned off—lurched and skidded around buttress roots. Its headlights swung in wild arcs across the trunks and down to the mud. Aerial creepers—great looping vines of them—swung down from the towering forest ceiling. A steady drip of condensation spattered the windshield, forcing Orne to use the wipers.

In the bucket seat of the sled's cab, Orne fought the controls. He was plagued by the vague slow-motion-floating sensation that a heavy planet native always feels in lighter gravity. It gave him an unhappy stomach.

Things skipped through the air around the lurching vehicle: flitting and darting things. Insects came in twin cones, siphoned toward the headlights. There was an endless chittering whistling tok-tok-toking in the gloom beyond the lights.

Stetson's voice hissed suddenly through the surgically implanted speaker: "How's it look?"

"Alien."

"Any sign of that mob?"

"Negative."

"O.K. We're taking off."

Behind Orne, there came a deep rumbling roar that receded as the scout cruiser climbed its jets. All other sounds hung suspended in after-silence, then resumed: the strongest first and then the weakest.

A heavy object suddenly arced through the headlights, swinging on a vine. It disappeared behind a tree. Another. Another. Ghostly shadows with vine pendulums on both sides. Something banged down heavily onto the hood of the sled.

Orne braked to a creaking stop that shifted the load behind him, found himself staring through

23

the windshield at a native of Gienah III. The native crouched on the hood, a Mark XX exploding-pellet rifle in his right hand directed at Orne's head. In the abrupt shock of meeting, Orne recognized the weapon: standard issue to the marine guards on all R&R survey ships.

The native appeared the twin of the one Orne had seen on the translite screen. The four-fingered hand looked extremely capable around the stock of the Mark XX.

Slowly, Orne put a hand to his throat, pressed the contact button. He moved his speaking muscles: *"Just made contact with the mob. One on the hood now has one of our Mark XX rifles aimed at my head."*

The surf-hissing of Stetson's voice came through the hidden speaker: *"Want us to come back?"*

"Negative. Stand by. He looks cautious rather than hostile."

Orne held up his right hand, palm out. He had a second thought: held up his left hand, too. Universal symbol of peaceful intentions: empty hands. The gun muzzle lowered slightly. Orne called into his mind the language that had been hypnoforced into him. *Ocheero? No. That means 'The People.' Ah*...And he had the heavy fricative greeting sound.

"Ffroiragrazzi," he said.

The native shifted to the left, answered in pure, un-accented High Galactese: "Who are you?"

Orne fought down a sudden panic. The lipless mouth had looked so odd forming the familiar words.

Stetson's voice hissed: *"Is that the native speaking Galactese?"*

Orne touched his throat. *"You heard him."*

He dropped his hand, said: "I am Lewis Orne of Rediscovery and Reeducation. I was sent here at the request of the First-Contact officer on the *Delphinus Rediscovery*."

"Where is your ship?" demanded the Gienahn.

"It put me down and left."

"Why?"

"It was behind schedule for another appointment."

Out of the corners of his eyes, Orne saw more shadows dropping to the mud around him. The sled shifted as someone climbed onto the load behind the cab. The someone scuttled agilely for a moment.

The native climbed down to the cab's side step, opened the door. The rifle was held at the ready. Again, the lipless mouth formed Galactese words: "What do you carry in this...vehicle?"

"The equipment every R&R field man uses to help the people of a rediscovered planet improve themselves." Orne nodded at the rifle. "Would you mind pointing that weapon some other direction? It makes me nervous."

The gun muzzle remained unwaveringly on Orne's middle. The native's mouth opened, revealing long canines. "Do we not look strange to you?"

"I take it there's been a heavy mutational variation in the humanoid norm on this planet," said Orne. "What is it? Hard radiation?"

No answer.

"It doesn't really make any difference, of course," said Orne. "I'm here to help you."

"I am Tanub, High Path Chief of the Grazzi," said the native. "I decide who is to help."

Orne swallowed.

"Where do you go?" demanded Tanub.

"I was hoping to go to your city. Is it permitted?"

A long pause while the vertical-slit pupils of Tanub's eyes expanded and contracted. "It is permitted."

Stetson's voice came through the hidden speaker: "All bets off. We're coming in after you. That Mark XX is the final straw. It means they have the *Delphinus* for sure!"

Orne touched his throat. *"No! Give me a little more time!"*

"Why?"

"I have a hunch about these creatures."

"What is it?"

"No time now. Trust me."

Another long pause in which Orne and Tanub continued to study each other. Presently, Stetson said: *"O.K. Go ahead as planned. But find out where the Delphinus is! If we get that back we pull their teeth."*

"Why do you keep touching your throat?" demanded Tanub.

"I'm nervous," said Orne. "Guns always make me nervous."

The muzzle lowered slightly.

"Shall we continue on to your city?" asked Orne. He wet his lips with his tongue. The cab light on Tanub's face was giving the Gienahn an eerie sinister look.

"We can go soon," said Tanub.

"Will you join me inside here?" asked Orne. "There's a passenger seat right behind me."

Tanub's eyes moved catlike: right, left. "Yes." He turned, barked an order into the jungle gloom, then climbed in behind Orne.

"When do we go?" asked Orne.

"The great sun will be down soon," said Tanub. "We can continue as soon as Chiranachuruso rises."

"Chiranachuruso?"

"Our satellite...our moon," said Tanub.

"It's a beautiful word," said Orne. "Chiranachuruso."

27

"In our tongue it means: The Limb of Victory," said Tanub. "By its light we will continue."

Orne turned, looked back at Tanub. "Do you mean to tell me that you can see by what light gets down here through those trees?"

"Can you not see?" asked Tanub.

"Not without the headlights."

"Our eyes differ," said Tanub. He bent toward Orne, peered. The vertical slit pupils of his eyes expanded, contracted. "You are the same as the...others."

"Oh, on the *Delphinus?*"

Pause. "Yes."

Presently, a greater gloom came over the jungle, bringing a sudden stillness to the wild life. There was a chittering commotion from the natives in the trees around the sled. Tanub shifted behind Orne.

"We may go now," he said. "Slowly...to stay behind my...scouts."

"Right." Orne eased the sled forward around an obstructing root.

Silence while they crawled ahead. Around them shapes flung themselves from vine to vine.

"I admired your city from the air," said Orne. "It is very beautiful."

"Yes," said Tanub. "Why did you land so far from it?"

"We didn't want to come down where we might de-stroy anything."

"There is nothing to destroy in the jungle," said Tanub.

"Why do you have such a big city?" asked Orne.

Silence.

"I said: Why do you—"

"You are ignorant of our ways," said Tanub. "There-fore, I forgive you. The city is for our race. We must breed and be born in sunlight. Once—long ago—we used crude platforms on the tops of the trees. Now... only the...wild ones do this."

Stetson's voice hissed in Orne's ears: *"Easy on the sex line, boy. That's always touchy. These crea-tures are oviparous. Sex glands are apparently hidden in that long fur behind where their chins ought to be."*

"Who controls the breeding sites controls our world," said Tanub. "Once there was another city. We de-stroyed it."

"Are there many...wild ones?" asked Orne.

"Fewer each year," said Tanub.

"There's how they get their slaves," hissed Stetson.

"You speak excellent Galactese," said Orne.

"The High Path Chief commanded the best teach-er," said Tanub. "Do you, too, know many things, Orne?"

"That's why I was sent here," said Orne.

29

"Are there many planets to teach?" asked Tanub.

"Very many," said Orne. "Your city—I saw very tall buildings. Of what do you build them?"

"In your tongue—glass," said Tanub. "The engineers of the *Delphinus* said it was impossible. As you saw—they are wrong."

"A glass-blowing culture," hissed Stetson. *"That'd explain a lot of things."*

Slowly, the disguised sled crept through the jungle. Once, a scout swooped down into the headlights, waved. Orne stopped on Tanub's order, and they waited almost ten minutes before proceeding.

"Wild ones?" asked Orne.

"Perhaps," said Tanub.

A glowing of many lights grew visible through the giant tree trunks. It grew brighter as the sled crept through the last of the jungle, emerged in cleared land at the edge of the city.

Orne stared upward in awe. The city fluted and spiraled into the moonlit sky. It was a fragile appearing lacery of bridges, winking dots of light. The bridges wove back and forth from building to building until the entire visible network appeared one gigantic dew-glittering web.

"All that with glass," murmured Orne.

"What's happening?" hissed Stetson.

Orne touched his throat contact. *"We're just into the city clearing, proceeding toward the nearest building."*

"This is far enough," said Tanub.

Orne stopped the sled. In the moonlight, he could see armed Gienahns all around. The buttressed pedestal of one of the buildings loomed directly ahead. It looked taller than had the scout cruiser in its jungle landing circle.

Tanub leaned close to Orne's shoulder. "We have not deceived you, have we, Orne?"

"Huh? What do you mean?"

"You have recognized that we are not mutated members of your race."

Orne swallowed. Into his ears came Stetson's voice: *"Better admit it."*

"That's true," said Orne.

"I like you, Orne," said Tanub. "You shall be one of my slaves. You will teach me many things."

"How did you capture the *Delphinus?*" asked Orne.

"You know that, too?"

"You have one of their rifles," said Orne.

"Your race is no match for us, Orne...in cunning, in strength, in the prowess of the mind. Your ship landed to repair its tubes. Very inferior ceramics in those tubes."

Orne turned, looked at Tanub in the dim glow of the cab light. "Have you heard about the I-A, Tanub?"

"I-A? What is that?" There was a wary tenseness in the Gienahn's figure. His mouth opened to reveal the long canines.

"You took the *Delphinus* by treachery?" asked Orne.

"They were simple fools," said Tanub. "We are smaller, thus they thought us weaker." The Mark XX's muzzle came around to center on Orne's stomach. "You have not answered my question. What is the I-A?"

"I am of the I-A," said Orne. "Where've you hidden the *Delphinus?*"

"In the place that suits us best," said Tanub. "In all our history there has never been a better place."

"What do you plan to do with it?" asked Orne.

"Within a year we will have a copy with our own improvements. After that—"

"You intend to start a war?" asked Orne.

"In the jungle the strong slay the weak until only the strong remain," said Tanub.

"And then the strong prey upon each other?" asked Orne.

"That is a quibble for women," said Tanub.

"It's too bad you feel that way," said Orne. "When two cultures meet like this they tend to help each other. What have you done with the crew of the *Delphinus?*"

"They are slaves," said Tanub. "Those who still live. Some resisted. Others objected to teaching us what we want to know." He waved the gun muzzle. "You will not be that foolish, will you, Orne?"

"No need to be," said Orne. "I've another little lesson to teach you: I already know where you've hidden the *Delphinus*."

"Go, boy!" hissed Stetson. *"Where is it?"*

"Impossible!" barked Tanub.

"It's on your moon," said Orne. "Darkside. It's on a mountain on the darkside of your moon."

Tanub's eyes dilated, contracted. "You read minds?"

"The I-A has no need to read minds," said Orne. "We rely on superior mental prowess."

"The marines are on their way," hissed Stetson. *"We're coming in to get you. I'm going to want to know how you guessed that one."*

"You are a weak fool like the others," gritted Tanub.

"It's too bad you formed your opinion of us by observing only the low grades of the R&R," said Orne.

"Easy, boy," hissed Stetson. *"Don't pick a fight with him now. Remember, his race is arboreal. He's probably as strong as an ape."*

"I could kill you where you sit!" grated Tanub.

"You write finish for your entire planet if you do," said Orne. "I'm not alone. There are others listening to every word we say. There's a ship overhead that could split open your planet with one bomb—wash it with molten rock. It'd run like the glass you use for your buildings."

"You are lying!"

"We'll make you an offer," said Orne. "We don't really want to exterminate you. We'll give you limited membership in the Galactic Federation until you prove you're no menace to us."

"Keep talking," hissed Stetson. *"Keep him interested."*

"You dare insult me!" growled Tanub.

"You had better believe me," said Orne. "We—"

Stetson's voice interrupted him: *"Got it, Orne! They caught the Delphinus on the ground right where you said it'd be! Blew the tubes off it. Marines now mopping up."*

"It's like this," said Orne. "We already have recaptured the *Delphinus.*" Tanub's eyes went instinctively skyward. "Except for the captured armament you still hold, you obviously don't have the weapons to meet us," continued Orne. "Otherwise, you wouldn't be carrying that rifle off the *Delphinus.*"

"If you speak the truth, then we shall die bravely," said Tanub.

"No need for you to die," said Orne.

"Better to die than be slaves," said Tanub.

"We don't need slaves," said Orne. "We—"

"I cannot take the chance that you are lying," said Tanub. "I must kill you now."

Orne's foot rested on the air sled control pedal. He depressed it. Instantly, the sled shot skyward, heavy G's pressing them down into the seats. The gun in Tanub's hands was slammed into his lap. He struggled to raise it. To Orne, the weight was still only about twice that of his home planet of Chargon. He reached over, took the rifle, found safety belts, bound Tanub with them. Then he eased off the acceleration.

"We don't need slaves," said Orne. "We have machines to do our work. We'll send experts in here, teach you people how to exploit your planet, how to build good transportation facilities, show you how to mine your minerals, how to—"

"And what do we do in return?" whispered Tanub.

"You could start by teaching us how you make superior glass," said Orne. "I certainly hope you see things our way. We really don't want to have to come down there and clean you out. It'd be a shame to have to blast that city into little pieces."

Tanub wilted. Presently, he said: "Send me back. I will discuss this with...our council." He stared at Orne. "You I-A's are too strong. We did not know."

In the wardroom of Stetson's scout cruiser, the lights were low, the leather chairs comfortable, the

35

green beige table set with a decanter of Hochar brandy and two glasses.

Orne lifted his glass, sipped the liquor, smacked his lips. "For a while there, I thought I'd never be tasting anything like this again."

Stetson took his own glass. "ComGO heard the whole thing over the general monitor net," he said. "D'you know you've been breveted to senior field man?"

"Ah, they've already recognized my sterling worth," said Orne.

The wolfish grin took over Stetson's big features. "Senior field men last about half as long as the juniors," he said. "Mortality's terrific?"

"I might've known," said Orne. He took another sip of the brandy.

Stetson flicked on the switch of a recorder beside him. "O.K. You can go ahead any time."

"Where do you want me to start?"

"First, how'd you spot right away where they'd hidden the *Delphinus?*"

"Easy. Tanub's word for his people was *Grazzi.* Most races call themselves something meaning *The People.* But in his tongue that's *Ocheero. Grazzi* wasn't on the translated list. I started working on it. The most likely answer was that it had been adopted from another language, and meant *enemy.*"

"And *that* told you where the *Delphinus* was?"

"No. But it fitted my hunch about these Gienahns. I'd kind of felt from the first minute of meeting them that they had a culture like the Indians of ancient Terra."

"Why?"

"They came in like a primitive raiding party. The leader dropped right onto the hood of my sled. An act of bravery, no less. Counting coup, you see?"

"I guess so."

"Then he said he was High Path Chief. That wasn't on the language list, either. But it was easy: *Raider Chief.* There's a word in almost every language in history that means raider and derives from a word for road, path or highway."

"Highwaymen," said Stetson.

"Raid itself," said Orne. "An ancient Terran language corruption of road."

"Yeah, yeah. But where'd all this translation griff put—"

"Don't be impatient. Glass-blowing culture meant they were just out of the primitive stage. That, we could control. Next, he said their moon was *Chiranachuruso,* translated as *The Limb of Victory.* After that it just fell into place."

"How?"

"The vertical-slit pupils of their eyes. Doesn't that mean anything to you?"

"Maybe. What's it mean to you?"

"Night-hunting predator accustomed to dropping upon its victims from above. No other type of creature ever has had the vertical slit. And Ta-nub said himself that the *Delphinus* was hidden in the best place in all of their history. History? That'd be a high place. Dark, likewise. Ergo: a high place on the darkside of their moon."

"I'm a pie-eyed greepus," whispered Stetson.

Orne grinned, said: "You probably are...sir."

OPERATION
HAYSTACK

It's hard to ferret out a gang of fanatics; it would, obviously, be even harder to spot a genetic line of dedicated men. But the problem Orne had was one step tougher than that!

WHEN THE INVESTIGATION & Adjustment scout cruiser landed on Marak it carried a man the doctors had no hope of saving. He was alive only because he was in a womblike creche pod that had taken over most of his vital functions.

The man's name was Lewis Orne. He had been a blocky, heavy-muscled redhead with slightly off-center features and the hard flesh of a heavy planet native. Even in the placid repose of near death there was something clownish about his appearance. His burned, ungent-covered face looked made up for some bizarre show.

Marak is the League capital, and the I-A medical center there is probably the best in the galaxy, but

43

it accepted the creche pod and Orne more as a curiosity than anything else. The man had lost one eye, three fingers of his left hand and part of his hair, suffered a broken jaw and various internal injuries. He had been in terminal shock for more than ninety hours.

Umbo Stetson, Orne's section chief, went back into his cruiser's "office" after a hospital flitter took pod and patient. There was an added droop to Stetson's shoulders that accentuated his usual slouching stance. His overlarge features were drawn into ridges of sorrow. A general straggling, trampish look about him was not helped by patched blue fatigues.

The doctor's words still rang in Stetson's ears: "This patient's vital tone is too low to permit operative replacement of damaged organs. He'll live for a while because of the pod, but—" And the doctor had shrugged.

Stetson slumped into his desk chair, looked out the open port beside him. Some four hundred meters below, the scurrying beetlelike activity of the I-A's main field sent up discordant roaring and clattering. Two rows of other scout cruisers were parked in line with Stetson's port—gleaming red and black needles. He stared at them without really seeing them.

It always happens on some "routine" assignment, he thought. Nothing but a slight suspicion about Heleb: the fact that only women held high office. One simple, unexplained fact...and I lose my best agent!

He sighed, turned to his desk, began composing the report:

"The militant core on the Planet Heleb has been eliminated. Occupation force on the ground. No further danger to Galactic peace expected from this source. Reason for operation: Rediscovery & Re-education—*after two years on the planet*—failed to detect signs of militancy. The major indications were: 1) a ruling caste restricted to women, and 2) disparity between numbers of males and females *far* beyond the Lutig norm! Senior Field Agent Lewis Orne found that the ruling caste was controlling the sex of offspring at conception (see attached details), and had raised a male slave army to maintain its rule. The R&R agent had been drained of information, then killed. Arms constructed on the basis of that information caused critical injuries to Senior Field Agent Orne. He is not expected to live. I am hereby urging that he receive the Galaxy Medal, and that his name be added to the Roll of Honor."

Stetson pushed the page aside. That was enough for ComGO, who never read anything but the first page anyway. Details were for his aides to chew and digest. They could wait. Stetson punched his desk callbox for Orne's service record, set himself to the task he most detested: notifying next of kin. He read, pursing his lips:

"Home Planet: Chargon. Notify in case of accident or death: Mrs. Victoria Orne, mother."

He leafed through the pages, reluctant to send the hated message. Orne had enlisted in the Marak

Marines at age seventeen—a runaway from home—
and his mother had given post-enlistment consent.
Two years later: scholarship transfer to Uni-Galacta, the R&R school here on Marak. Five years
of school and one R&R field assignment under his
belt, and he had been drafted into the I-A for bril-
liant detection of militancy on Hammel. And two
years later—*kaput!*

Abruptly, Stetson hurled the service record at the
gray metal wall across from him; then he got up,
brought the record back to his desk, smoothing the
pages. There were tears in his eyes. He flipped a
switch on his desk, dictated the notification to Central Secretarial, ordered it sent out priority. Then he
went groundside and got drunk on Hochar Brandy,
Orne's favorite drink.

The next morning there was a reply from Chargon:
"Lewis Orne's mother too ill to travel. Sisters being
notified. Please ask Mrs. Ipscott Bullone of Marak,
wife of the High Commissioner, to take over for
family." It was signed: "Madrena Orne Standish,
sister."

With some misgivings, Stetson called the residence
of Ipscott Bullone, leader of the majority party in
the Marak Assembly. Mrs. Bullone took the call
with blank screen. There was a sound of running
water in the background. Stetson stared at the
grayness swimming in his desk visor. He always
disliked a blank screen. A baritone husk of a voice
slid: "This is Polly Bullone."

Stetson introduced himself, relayed the Chargon message.

"Victoria's boy dying? Here? Oh, the poor thing! And Madrena's back on Chargon...the election. Oh, yes, of course. I'll get right over to the hospital!"

Stetson signed off, broke the contact.

The High Commissioner's wife yet! he thought. Then, because he had to do it, he walled off his sorrow, got to work.

At the medical center, the oval creche containing Orne hung from ceiling hooks in a private room. There were humming sounds in the dim, watery greenness of the room, rhythmic chuggings, sighings. Occasionally, a door opened almost soundlessly, and a white-clad figure would check the graph tapes on the creche's meters.

Orne was lingering. He became the major conversation piece at the internes' coffee breaks: "That agent who was hurt on Heleb, he's still with us. Man, they must build those guys different from the rest of us!... Yeah! Understand he's got only about an eighth of his insides...liver, kidneys, stomach—all gone...Lay you odds he doesn't last out the month...Look what old sure-thing McTavish wants to bet on!"

On the morning of his eighty-eighth day in the creche, the day nurse came into Orne's room, lifted the inspection hood, looked down at him. The day nurse was a tall, lean-faced professional who had learned to meet miracles and failures with equal lack of expression. However, this routine with the dying I-A operative had lulled her into a state of

47

psychological unpreparedness. *Any day now, poor guy,* she thought. And she gasped as she opened his sole remaining eye, said:

"Did they clobber those dames on Heleb?"

"Yes, sir!" she blurted. "They really did, sir!"

"Good!"

Orne closed his eye. His breathing deepened.

The nurse rang frantically for the doctors.

It had been an indeterminate period in a blank fog for Orne, then a time of pain and the gradual realization that he was in a creche. Had to be. He could remember his sudden exposure on Heleb, the explosion—then nothing. Good old creche. It made him feel safe now, shielded from all danger.

Orne began to show minute but steady signs of improvement. In another month, the doctors ventured an intestinal graft that gave him a new spurt of energy. Two months later, they replaced missing eye and fingers, restored his scalp line, worked artistic surgery on his burn scars.

Fourteen months, eleven days, five hours and two minutes after he had been picked up "as good as dead," Orne walked out of the hospital under his own power, accompanied by a strangely silent Umbo Stetson.

Under the dark blue I-A field cape, Orne's coverall uniform fitted his once muscular frame like a deflated bag. But the pixie light had returned to his eyes—even to the eye he had received from a nameless and long dead donor. Except for the loss of weight, he looked to be the same Lewis Orne. If he was different—beyond the "spare parts"—it was something he only suspected, something that made the idea, "twice-born," not a joke.

Outside the hospital, clouds obscured Marak's green sun. It was midmorning. A cold spring wind bent the pile lawn, tugged fitfully at the border plantings of exotic flowers around the hospital's landing pad.

Orne paused on the steps above the pad, breathed deeply of the chill air. "Beautiful day," he said.

Stetson reached out a hand to help Orne down the steps, hesitated, put the hand back in his pocket. Beneath the section chief's look of weary superciliousness there was a note of anxiety. His big features were set in a frown. The drooping eyelids failed to conceal a sharp, measuring stare.

Orne glanced at the sky to the southwest. "The flitter ought to be here any minute." A gust of wind tugged at his cape. He staggered, caught his balance. "I *feel* good."

"You look like something left over from a funeral," growled Stetson.

"Sure—my funeral," said Orne. He grinned. "Anyway, I was getting tired of that walk-around-type morgue. All my nurses were married."

"I'd almost stake my life that I could trust you," muttered Stetson.

49

Orne looked at him. "No, no, Stet...stake *my* life. I'm used to it."

Stetson shook his head. "No, dammit! I trust you, but you deserve a peaceful convalescence. We've no right to saddle you with—"

"Stet?" Orne's voice was low, amused.

"Huh?" Stetson looked up.

"Let's save the noble act for someone who doesn't know you," said Orne. "You've a job for me. O.K. You've made the gesture for your conscience."

Stetson produced a wolfish grin. "All right. So we're desperate, and we haven't much time. In a nutshell, since you're going to be a house guest at the Bullones'—we suspect Ipscott Bullone of being the head of a conspiracy to take over the government."

"What do you mean—*take over the government?*" demanded Orne. "The Galactic High Commissioner *is* the government—subject to the Constitution and the Assemblymen who elected him."

"We've a situation that could explode into another Rim War, and we think he's at the heart of it," said Stetson. "We've eighty-one touchy planets, all of them old-line steadies that have been in the League for years. And on every one of them we have reason to believe there's a clan of traitors sworn to overthrow the League. Even on your home planet—Chargon."

"You want me to go home for my convalescence?" asked Orne. "Haven't been there since I was seventeen. I'm not sure that—"

"No, dammit! We want you as the Bullones' house guest! And speaking of that, would you mind explaining how they were chosen to ride herd on you?"

"There's an odd thing," said Orne. "All those gags in the I-A about old Upshook Ipscott Bullone...and then I find that his wife went to school with my mother."

"Have you met Himself?"

"He brought his wife to the hospital a couple of times."

Again, Stetson looked to the southwest, then back to Orne. A pensive look came over his face. "Every schoolkid knows how the Nathians and the Marakian League fought it out in the Rim War—how the old civilization fell apart—and it all seems kind of distant," he said.

"Five hundred standard years," said Orne.

"And maybe no farther away than yesterday," murmured Stetson. He cleared his throat.

And Orne wondered why Stetson was moving so cautiously. *Something deep troubling him.* A sudden thought struck Orne. He said: "You spoke of trust. Has this conspiracy involved the I-A?"

"We think so," said Stetson. "About a year ago, an R&R archeological team was nosing around some ruins on Dabih. The place was all but vitrified in the Rim War, but a whole bank of records from a

51

Nathian outpost escaped." He glanced sidelong at Orne. "The Rah&Rah boys couldn't make sense out of the records. No surprise. They called in an I-A crypt-analyst. He broke a complicated substitution cipher. When the stuff started making sense he pushed the panic button."

"For something the Nathians wrote five hundred years ago?"

Stetson's drooping eyelids lifted. There was a cold quality to his stare. "This was a routing station for key Nathian families," he said. "Trained refugees. An old dodge...been used as long as there've been—"

"But five hundred *years*, Stet!"

"I don't care if it was five *thousand* years!" barked Stetson. "We've intercepted some scraps since then that were written in the *same* code. The bland confidence of *that!* Wouldn't that gall you?" He shook his head. "And every scrap we've intercepted deals with the coming elections."

"But the election's only a couple of days off!" protested Orne.

Stetson glanced at his wristchrono. "Forty-two hours to be exact," he said. "Some deadline!"

"Any names in these old records?" asked Orne.

Stetson nodded. "Names of planets, yes. People, no. Some code names, but no cover names. Code name on Chargon was *Winner*. That ring any bells with you?"

Orne shook his head. "No. What's the code name here?"

"The Head," said Stetson. "But what good does that do us? They're sure to've changed those by now."

"They didn't change their communications code," said Orne.

"No...they didn't."

"We must have something on them, some leads," said Orne. He felt that Stetson was holding back something vital.

"Sure," said Stetson. "We have history books. They say the Nathians were top drawer in political mechanics. We know for a fact they chose landing sites for their *refugees* with diabolical care. Each family was told to dig in, grow up with the adopted culture, develop the weak spots, build an underground, train their descendants to take over. They set out to bore from within, to make victory out of defeat. The Nathians were long on patience. They came originally from nomad stock on Nathia II. Their mythology calls them Arbs or Ayrbs. Go review your seventh grade history. You'll know almost as much as we do!"

"Like looking for the traditional needle in the haystack," muttered Orne. "How come you suspect High Commissioner Upshook?"

Stetson wet his lips with his tongue. "One of the Bullones' seven daughters is currently at home," he said. "Name's Diana. A field leader in the I-A women. One of the Nathian code messages we intercepted had her name as addressee."

"Who sent the message?" asked Orne. "What was it all about?"

Stetson coughed. "You know, Lew, we cross-check everything. This message was signed M.O.S. The only M.O.S. that came out of the comparison was on a routine next-of-kin reply. We followed it down to the original copy, and the handwriting checked. Name of Madrena Orne Standish."

"Maddie?" Orne froze, turned slowly to face Stetson. "So that's what's troubling you!"

"We know you haven't been home since you were seventeen," said Stetson. "Your record with us is clean. The question is—"

"Permit me," said Orne. "The question is: Will I turn in my own sister if it falls that way?"

Stetson remained silent, staring at him.

"O.K.," said Orne. "My job is seeing that we don't have another Rim War. Just answer me one question: How's Maddie mixed up in this? My family isn't one of these traitor clans."

"This whole thing is all tangled up with politics," said Stetson. "We think it's because of her husband."

"Ahhhh, the member for Chargon," said Orne. "I've never met him." He looked to the southwest where a flitter was growing larger as it approached. "Who's my cover contact?"

"That mini-transceiver we planted in your neck for the Gienah job," said Stetson. "It's still there and functioning. Anything happens around you, we hear it."

Orne touched the subvocal stud at his neck, moved his speaking muscles without opening his mouth. A surf-hissing voice filled the matching transceiver in Stetson's neck:

"You pay attention while I'm making a play for this Diana Bullone, you hear? Then you'll know how an expert works."

"Don't get so interested in your work that you forget why you're out there," growled Stetson.

Mrs. Bullone was a fat little mouse of a woman. She stood almost in the center of the guest room of her home, hands clasped across the paunch of a long, dull silver gown. She had demure gray eyes, grandmotherly gray hair combed straight back in a jeweled net—and that shocking baritone husk of a voice issuing from a small mouth. Her figure sloped out from several chins to a matronly bosom, then dropped straight like a barrel. The top of her head came just above Orne's dress epaulets.

"We want you to feel at home here, Lewis," she husked. "You're to consider yourself one of the family."

Orne looked around at the Bullone guest room: low key furnishings with an old-fashioned selectacol for change of decor. A polawindow looked out onto an oval swimming pool, the glass muted to dark blue. It gave the outside a moonlight appearance. There was a contour bed against one wall, several built-ins, and a door partly open to reveal bathroom tiles. Everything traditional and comfortable.

"I already *do* feel at home," he said. "You know, your house is very like our place on Chargon. I was surprised when I saw it from the air. Except for the setting, it looks almost identical."

"I guess your mother and I shared ideas when we were in school," said Polly. "We were *very* close friends."

"You must've been to do all this for me," said Orne. "I don't know how I'm ever going to—"

"Ah! Here we are!" A deep masculine voice boomed from the open door behind Orne. He turned, saw Ipscott Bullone, High Commissioner of the Marakian League. Bullone was tall, had a face of harsh angles and deep lines, dark eyes under heavy brows, black hair trained in receding waves. There was a look of ungainly clumsiness about him.

He doesn't strike me as the dictator type, thought Orne. *But that's obviously what Stet suspects.*

"Glad you made it out all right, son," boomed Bullone. He advanced into the room, glanced around. "Hope everything's to your taste here."

"Lewis was just telling me that our place is very like his mother's home on Chargon," said Polly.

"It's old fashioned, but we like it," said Bullone. "Just a great big tetragon on a central pivot. We can turn any room we want to the sun, the shade or the breeze, but we usually leave the main salon pointing northeast. View of the capital, you know."

"We have a sea breeze on Chargon that we treat the same way," said Orne.

56

"I'm sure Lewis would like to be left alone for a while now," said Polly. "This is his first day out of the hospital. We mustn't tire him." She crossed to the polawindow, adjusted it to neutral gray, turned the selectacol, and the room's color dominance shifted to green. "There, that's more restful," she said. "Now, if there's anything you need you just ring the bell there by your bed. The autobutle will know where to find us."

The Bullones left, and Orne crossed to the window, looked out at the pool. The young woman hadn't come back. When the chauffeur-driven limousine flitter had dropped down to the house's landing pad, Orne had seen a parasol and sunhat nodding to each other on the blue tiles beside the pool. The parasol had shielded Polly Bullone. The sunhat had been worn by a shapely young woman in swimming tights, who had rushed off into the house.

She was no taller than Polly, but slender and with golden red hair caught under the sunhat in a swimmer's chignon. She was not beautiful—face too narrow with suggestions of Bullone's cragginess, and the eyes overlarge. But her mouth was full-lipped, chin strong, and there had been an air of exquisite assurance about her. The total effect had been one of striking elegance—extremely feminine.

Orne looked beyond the pool: wooded hills and, dimly on the horizon, a broken line of mountains. The Bullones lived in expensive isolation. Around them stretched miles of wilderness, rugged with planned neglect.

Time to report in, he thought. Orne pressed the neck stud on his transceiver, got Stetson, told him what had happened to this point.

"All right," said Stetson. "Go find the daughter. She fits the description of the gal you saw by the pool."

"That's what I was hoping," said Orne.

He changed into light-blue fatigues, went to the door of his room, let himself out into a hall. A glance at his wristchrono showed that it was shortly before noon—time for a bit of scouting before they called lunch. He knew from his brief tour of the house and its similarity to the home of his childhood that the hall let into the main living salon. The public rooms and men's quarters were in the outside ring. Secluded family apartments and women's quarters occupied the inner section.

Orne made his way to the salon. It was long, built around two sections of the tetragon, and with low divans beneath the view windows. The floor was thick pile rugs pushed one against another in a crazy patchwork of reds and browns. At the far end of the room, someone in blue fatigues like his own was bent over a stand of some sort. The figure straightened at the same time a tinkle of music filled the room. He recognized the red-gold hair of the young woman he had seen beside the pool. She was wielding two mallets to play a stringed instrument that lay on its side supported by a carved-wood stand.

He moved up behind her, his footsteps muffled by the carpeting. The music had a curious rhythm that suggested figures dancing wildly around firelight. She struck a final chord, muted the strings.

"That makes me homesick," said Orne.

"Oh!" She whirled, gasped, then smiled. "You startled me. I thought I was alone."

"Sorry. I was enjoying the music."

"I'm Diana Bullone," she said. "You're Mr. Orne."

"Lew to all of the Bullone family, I hope," he said.

"Of course...Lew." She gestured at the musical instrument. "This is very old. Most find its music... well, rather weird. It's been handed down for generations in mother's family."

"The kaithra," said Orne. "My sisters play it. Been a long time since I've heard one."

"Oh, of course," she said. "Your mother's—" She stopped, looked confused. "I've got to get used to the fact that you're...I mean that we have a strange man around the house who isn't *exactly* strange."

Orne grinned. In spite of the blue I-A fatigues and a rather severe pulled-back hairdo, this was a handsome woman. He found himself liking her, and this caused him a feeling near self-loathing. She was a suspect. He couldn't afford to like her. But the Bullones were being so decent, taking him in like this. And how was their hospitality being repaid? By spying and prying. Yet, his first loyalty belonged to the I-A, to the peace it represented.

He said rather lamely: "I hope you get over the feeling that I'm strange."

"I'm over it already," she said. She linked arms with him, said: "If you feel up to it, I'll take you on the deluxe guided tour."

By nightfall, Orne was in a state of confusion. He had found Diana fascinating, and yet the most comfortable woman to be around that he had ever met. She liked swimming, *paloika* hunting, *ditar* apples—She had a "poo-poo" attitude toward the older generation that she said she'd never before revealed to anyone. They had laughed like fools over utter nonsense.

Orne went back to his room to change for dinner, stopped before the polawindow. The quick darkness of these low latitudes had pulled an ebon blanket over the landscape. There was city-glow off to the left, and an orange halo to the peaks where Marak's three moons would rise. *Am I falling in love with this woman?* he asked himself. He felt like calling Stetson, not to report but just to talk the situation out. And this made him acutely aware that Stetson or an aide had heard everything said between them that afternoon.

The autobutle called dinner. Orne changed hurriedly into a fresh lounge uniform, found his way to the small salon across the house. The Bullones already were seated around an old-fashioned bubble-slot table set with real candles, golden *shardi* service. Two of Marak's moons could be seen out the window climbing swiftly over the peaks.

"You turned the house," said Orne.

"We like the moonrise," said Polly. "It seems more romantic, don't you think?" She glanced at Diana.

Diana looked down at her plate. She was wearing a low-cut gown of *firemesh* that set off her red hair. A single strand of *Reinach* pearls gleamed at her throat.

Orne sat down in the vacant seat opposite her. *What a handsome woman!* he thought.

Polly, on Orne's right, looked younger and softer in a green stola gown that hazed her barrel contours. Bullone, across from her, wore black lounging shorts and knee-length *kubi* jacket of golden pearl cloth. Everything about the people and setting reeked of wealth, power. For a moment, Orne saw that Stetson's suspicions could have basis in fact. Bullone might go to any lengths to maintain this luxury.

Orne's entrance had interrupted an argument between Polly and her husband. They welcomed him, went right on without inhibition. Rather than embarrassing him, this made him feel more at home, more accepted.

"But I'm not running for office this time," said Bullone patiently. "Why do we have to clutter up the evening with that many people just to—"

"Our election night parties are traditional," said Polly.

"Well, I'd just like to relax quietly at home tomorrow," he said. "Take it easy with just the family here and not have to—"

"It's not like it was a *big* party," said Polly. "I've kept the list to fifty."

Diana straightened, said: "This is an important election Daddy! How could you *possibly* relax? There're seventy-three seats in question...the whole balance. If things go wrong in just the Alkes sector...why... you could be sent back to the floor. You'd lose your job as...why...someone else could take over as—"

"Welcome to the job," said Bullone. "It's a headache." He grinned at Orne. "Sorry to burden you with this, m'boy, but the women of this family run me ragged. I guess from what I hear that you've had a pretty busy day, too." He smiled paternally at Diana. "And your first day out of the hospital."

"She sets quite a pace, but I've enjoyed it," said Orne.

"We're taking the small flitter for a tour of the wilderness area tomorrow," said Diana. "Lew can relax all the way. I'll do the driving."

"Be sure you're back in plenty of time for the party," said Polly. "Can't have—" She broke off at a low bell from the alcove behind her. "That'll be for me. Excuse me, please...no, don't get up."

Orne bent to his dinner as it came out of the bubble slot beside his plate: meat in an exotic sauce, *Sirik* champagne, *paloika au semil*...more luxury.

Presently, Polly returned, resumed her seat.

"Anything important?" asked Bullone.

"Only a cancellation for tomorrow night. Professor Wingard is ill."

"I'd just as soon it was cancelled down to the four of us," said Bullone.

Unless this is a pose, this doesn't sound like a man who wants to grab more power, thought Orne.

"Scottie, you should take more pride in your office!" snapped Polly. "You're an important man."

"If it weren't for you, I'd be a nobody and prefer it," said Bullone. He grinned at Orne. "I'm a political idiot compared to my wife. Never saw anyone who could call the turn like she does. Runs in her family. Her mother was the same way."

Orne stared at him, fork raised from plate and motionless. A sudden idea had exploded in his mind.

"You must know something of this life, Lewis," said Bullone. "Your father was member for Chargon once, wasn't he?"

"Yes," murmured Orne. "But that was before I was born. He died in office." He shook his head, thought: *It couldn't be...but—*

"Do you feel all right, Lew?" asked Diana. "You're suddenly so pale."

"Just tired," said Orne. "Guess I'm not used to so much activity."

"And I've been a beast keeping you so busy today," she said.

"Don't you stand on ceremony here, son," said Polly. She looked concerned. "You've been very sick, and we understand. If you're tired, you go right on into bed."

Orne glanced around the table, met anxious attention in each face. He pushed his chair back, said: "Well, if you really don't mind—"

"Mind!" barked Polly. "You scoot along now!"

"See you in the morning. Lew," said Diana.

He nodded, turned away, thinking: *What a handsome woman!* As he started down the hall, he heard Bullone say to Diana: "Di, perhaps you'd better not take that boy out tomorrow. After all, he *is* supposed to be here for a rest." Her answer was lost as Orne entered the hall, closed the door.

In the privacy of his room, Orne pressed the transceiver stud at his neck, said: *"Stet?"*

A voice hissed in his ears: *"This is Mr. Stetson's relief. Orne, isn't it?"*

"Yes. I want a check right away on those Nathian records the archaeologists found. Find out if Heleb was one of the planets they seeded."

"Right. Hang on." There was a long silence, then: *"Lew, this is Stet. How come the question about Heleb?"*

"Was it on that Nathian list?"

"Negative. Why'd you ask?"

"Are you sure, Stet? It'd explain a lot of things."

"It's not on the lists, but...wait a minute." Silence. Then: *"Heleb was on line of flight to Auriga, and*

Auriga was on the list. We've reason to doubt they put anyone down on Auriga. If their ship ran into trouble—"

"*That's it!*" snapped Orne.

"*Keep your voice down or talk subvocally.*" ordered Stetson. "*Now, answer my question: What's up?*"

"*Something so fantastic it frightens me,*" said Orne. "*Remember that the women who ruled Heleb bred female or male children by controlling the sex of their offspring at conception. The method was unique. In fact, our medics thought it was impossible until—*"

"*You don't have to remind me of something we want buried and forgotten,*" interrupted Stetson. "*Too much chance for misuse of that formula.*"

"*Yes,*" said Orne. "*But what if your Nathian underground is composed entirely of women bred the same way? What if the Heleb women were just a bunch who got out of hand because they'd lost contact with the main element?*"

"*Holy Moley!*" blurted Stetson. "*Do you have evidence—*"

"*Nothing but a hunch,*" said Orne. "*Do you have a list of the guests who'll be here for the election party tomorrow?*"

"*We can get it. Why?*"

"*Check for women who mastermind their husbands in politics. Let me know how many and who.*"

"*Lew, that's not enough to—*"

"That's all I can give you for now, but I think I'll have more. Remember that..." he hesitated, spacing his words as a new thought struck him *"...the... Nathians...were...nomads."*

Day began early for the Bullones. In spite of its being election day, Bullone took off for his office an hour after dawn. "See what I mean about this job owning you?" he asked Orne.

"We're going to take it easy today, Lew," said Diana. She took his hand as they came up the steps after seeing her father to his limousine flitter. The sky was cloudless.

Orne felt himself liking her hand in his—liking the feel of it too much. He withdrew his hand, stood aside, said: "Lead on."

I've got to watch myself, he thought. *She's too charming.*

"I think a picnic," said Diana. "There's a little lake with grassy banks off to the west. We'll take viewers and a couple of good novels. This'll be a do-nothing day."

Orne hesitated. There might be things going on at the house that he should watch. But no...if he was right about this situation, then Diana could be the weak link. Time was closing in on them, too. By tomorrow the Nathians could have the government completely under control.

It was warm beside the lake. There were purple and orange flowers above the grassy bank. Small creatures flitted and cheeped in the brush and trees. There was a *groomis* in the reeds at the lower end of the lake, and every now and then it honked like an old man clearing his throat.

"When we girls were all at home we used to picnic here every Eight-day," said Diana. She lay on her back on the groundmat they'd spread. Orne sat beside her facing the lake. "We made a raft over there on the other side," she said. She sat up, looked across the lake. "You know, I think pieces of it are still there. See?" She pointed at a jumble of logs. As she gestured, her hand brushed Orne's.

Something like an electric shock passed between them. Without knowing exactly how it happened, Orne found his arms around Diana, their lips pressed together in a lingering kiss. Panic was very close to the surface in Orne. He broke away.

"I didn't plan for that to happen," whispered Diana.

"Nor I," muttered Orne. He shook his head. "Sometimes things can get into an awful mess!"

Diana blinked. "Lew...don't you...like me?"

He ignored the monitoring transceiver, spoke his mind. *They'll just think it's part of the act*, he thought. And the thought was bitter.

"Like you?" he asked. "I think I'm in love with you!"

She sighed, leaned against his shoulder. "Then what's wrong? You're not already married. Mother had your service record checked." Diana smiled impishly. "Mother has second sight."

The bitterness was like a sour taste in Orne's mouth. He could see the pattern so clearly. "Di, I ran away from home when I was seventeen," he said.

"I know, darling. Mother's told me all about you."

"You don't understand," he said. "My father died before I was born. He—"

"It must've been very hard on your mother," she said. "Left all alone with her family...and a new baby on the way."

"They'd known for a long time," said Orne. "My father had *Broach's* disease, and they found out too late. It was already in the central nervous system."

"How horrible," whispered Diana.

Orne's mind felt suddenly like a fish out of water. He found himself grasping at a thought that flopped around just out of reach. "Dad was in politics," he whispered. He felt as though he were living in a dream. His voice stayed low, shocked. "From when I first began to talk, Mother started grooming me to take his place in public life."

"And you didn't like politics," said Diana.

"I hated it!" he growled. "First chance, I ran away. One of my sisters married a young fellow who's now the member for Chargon. I hope he enjoys it!"

"That'd be Maddie," said Diana.

"You know her?" asked Orne. Then he remembered what Stetson had told him, and the thought was chilling.

"Of course I know her," said Diana. "Lew, what's wrong with you?"

"You'd expect me to play the same game, you calling the shots," he said. "Shoot for the top, cut and scramble, claw and dig."

"By tomorrow all that may not be necessary," she said.

Orne heard the sudden hiss of the carrier wave in his neck transceiver, but there was no voice from the monitor.

"What's...happening...tomorrow?" he asked.

"The election, silly," she said. "Lew, you're acting very strangely. Are you sure you're feeling all right." She put a hand to his forehead. "Perhaps we'd—"

"Just a minute," said Orne. "About us—" He swallowed.

She withdrew her hand. "I think my parents already suspect. We Bullones are notorious love-at-first-sighters." Her overlarge eyes studied him fondly. "You don't feel feverish, but maybe we'd better—"

"What a dope I am!" snarled Orne. "I just realized that I have to be a Nathian, too."

"You *just* realized?" She stared at him.

There was a hissing gasp in Orne's transceiver.

"The identical patterns in our families," he said. "Even to the houses. And there's the real key. What a dope!" He snapped his fingers. "*The head!* Polly! Your mother's the grand boss woman, isn't she?"

"But, darling...of course. She—"

"You'd better take me to her and fast!" snapped Orne. He touched the stud at his neck, but Stetson's voice intruded.

"*Great work, Lew! We're moving in a special shock force. Can't take any chances with—*"

Orne spoke aloud in panic: "*Stet! You get out to the Bullones! And you get there alone! No troops!*"

Diana had jumped to her feet, backed away from him.

"*What do you mean?*" demanded Stetson.

"*I'm saving our stupid necks!*" barked Orne. "*Alone! You hear? Or we'll have a worse mess on our hands than any Rim War!*"

There was an extended silence. "*You hear me, Stet?*" demanded Orne.

"*O.K., Lew. We're putting the O-force on standby. I'll be at the Bullones' in ten minutes. ComGO will be with me.*" Pause. "*And you'd better know what you're doing!*"

It was an angry group in a corner of the Bullones' main salon. Louvered shades cut the green glare of a noon sun. In the background there was the hum of air-conditioning and the clatter of roboservants preparing for the night's election party. Stetson leaned against the wall beside a divan, hands jammed deeply into the pockets of his wrinkled, patched fatigues. The wagon tracks furrowed his high forehead. Near Stetson, Admiral Sobat Spencer, the I-A's Commander of Galactic Operations, paced the floor. ComGO was a bull-necked bald man with wide blue eyes, a deceptively mild voice. There was a caged animal look to his pacing—three steps out, three steps back.

Polly Bullone sat on the divan. Her mouth was pulled into a straight line. Her hands were clasped so tightly in her lap that the knuckles showed white. Diana stood beside her mother. Her fists were clenched at her sides. She shivered with fury. Her gaze remained fixed, glaring at Orne.

"O.K., so my stupidity set up this little meeting," snarled Orne. He stood about five paces in front of Polly, hands on hips. The admiral, pacing away at his right, was beginning to wear on his nerves. "But you'd better listen to what I have to say." He glanced at the ComGO. "*All* of you."

Admiral Spencer stopped pacing, glowered at Orne. "I have yet to hear a good reason for not tearing this place apart...getting to the bottom of this situation."

"You...traitor, Lewis!" husked Polly.

"I'm inclined to agree with you, Madame," said Spencer. "Only from a different point of view." He glanced at Stetson. "Any word yet on Scottie Bullone?"

"They were going to call me the minute they found him," said Stetson. His voice sounded cautious, brooding.

"You were coming to the party here tonight, weren't you, admiral?" asked Orne.

"What's that have to do with anything?" demanded Spencer.

"Are you prepared to jail your wife and daughters for conspiracy?" asked Orne.

A tight smile played around Polly's lips.

Spencer opened his mouth, closed it soundlessly.

"The Nathians are mostly women," said Orne. "There's evidence that your womenfolk are among them."

The admiral looked like a man who had been kicked in the stomach. "What...evidence?" he whispered.

"I'll come to that in a moment," said Orne. "Now, note this: the Nathians are mostly women. There were only a few *accidents* and a few planned males, like me. That's why there were no family names to trace—just a tight little female society, all working to positions of power through their men."

Spencer cleared his throat, swallowed. He seemed powerless to take his attention from Orne's mouth.

"My guess," said Orne, "is that about thirty or forty years ago, the conspirators first began breeding a few males, grooming them for really choice top positions. Other Nathian males—the accidents where sex-control failed—they never learned about

72

the conspiracy. These new ones were full-fledged members. That's what I'd have been if I'd panned out as expected."

Polly glared at him, looked back at her hands.

"That part of the plan was scheduled to come to a head with this election," said Orne. "If they pulled this one off, they could move in more boldly."

"You're in way over your head, boy," growled Polly. "You're too late to do anything about us!"

"We'll see about that!" barked Spencer. He seemed to have regained his self-control. "A little publicity in the right places...some key arrests and—"

"No," said Orne. "She's right. It's too late for that. It was probably too late a hundred years ago. These dames were too firmly entrenched even then."

Stetson straightened away from the wall, smiled grimly at Orne. He seemed to be understanding a point that the others were missing. Diana still glared at Orne. Polly kept her attention on her hands, the tight smile playing about her lips.

"These women probably control one out of three of the top positions in the League," said Orne. "Maybe more. Think, admiral...think what would happen if you exposed this thing. There'd be secessions, riots, sub-governments would topple, the central government would be torn by suspicions and battles. What breeds in that atmosphere?" He shook his head. "The Rim War would seem like a picnic!"

"We can't just ignore this!" barked Spencer. He stiffened, glared at Orne.

"We can and we will," said Orne. "No choice."

Polly looked up, studied Orne's face. Diana looked confused.

"Once a Nathian, always a Nathian, eh?" snarled Spencer.

"There's no such thing," said Orne. "Five hundred years' cross-breeding with other races saw to that. There's merely a secret society of astute political scientists." He smiled wryly at Polly, glanced back at Spencer. "Think of your own wife, sir. In all honesty, would you be ComGO today if she hadn't guided your career?"

Spencer's face darkened. He drew in his chin, tried to stare Orne down, failed. Presently, he chuckled wryly.

"Sobie is beginning to come to his senses," said Polly. "You're about through, son."

"Don't underestimate your future son-in-law," said Orne.

"Hah!" barked Diana. "I *hate* you, Lewis Orne!"

"You'll get over that," said Orne mildly.

"Ohhhhhh!" Diana quivered with fury.

"My major point is this," said Orne. "Government is a dubious glory. You pay for your power and wealth by balancing on the sharp edge of the blade. That great amorphous thing out there—the people—has turned and swallowed many governments. The only way you can stay in power is by giving *good* government. Otherwise—sooner on later—your turn comes. I can remember my mother making that point. It's one of the things that stuck with me." He frowned. "My objection to politics is the compromises you have to make to get elected!"

Stetson moved out from the wall. "It's pretty clear," he said. Heads turned toward him. "To stay in power, the Nathians had to give us a fairly good government. On the other hand, if we expose them, we give a bunch of political amateurs—every fanatic and power-hungry demagogue in the galaxy—just the weapon they need to sweep them into office."

"After that: chaos," said Orne. "So we let the Nathians continue...with two minor alterations."

"We alter nothing," said Polly. "It occurs to me, Lewis, that you don't have a leg to stand on. You have me, but you'll get nothing out of me. The rest of the organization can go on without me. You don't dare expose us. We hold the whip hand!"

"The I-A could have ninety per cent of your organization in custody inside of ten days," said Orne.

"You couldn't find them!" snapped Polly.

"How?" asked Stetson.

"Nomads," said Orne. "This house is a glorified tent. Men on the outside, women on the inside. Look for inner courtyard construction. It's instinctive with Nathian blood. Add to that, an inclination for odd musical instruments—the kaithra, the tambour,

75

the oboe—all nomad instruments. Add to that, female dominance of the family—an odd twist on the nomad heritage, but not completely unique. Check for predominance of female offspring. Dig into political background. We'll miss damn few!"

Polly just stared at him, mouth open.

Spencer said: "Things are moving too fast for me. I know just one thing: I'm dedicated to preventing another Rim War. If I have to jail every last one of—"

"An hour after this conspiracy became known, you wouldn't be in a position to jail anyone," said Orne. "The husband of a Nathian! You'd be in jail yourself or more likely dead at the hands of a mob!"

Spencer paled.

"What's your suggestion for compromise?" asked Polly.

"Number one: the I-A gets veto power on any candidate you put up," said Orne. "Number two: you can never hold more than two thirds of the top offices."

"Who in the I-A vetoes our candidates?" asked Polly.

"Admiral Spencer, Stet, myself...anyone else we deem trustworthy," said Orne.

"You think you're a god or something?" demanded Polly.

"No more than you do," said Orne. "This is what's known as a check and balance system. You cut the pie. We get first choice on which pieces to take."

There was a protracted silence; then Spencer said: "It doesn't seem right just to—"

"No political compromise is ever totally right," said Polly. "You keep patching up things that always have flaws in them. That's how government is." She chuckled, looked up at Orne. "All right, Lewis. We accept." She glanced at Spencer, who shrugged, nodded glumly. Polly looked back at Orne. "Just answer me one question: How'd you know I was boss lady?"

"Easy," said Orne. "The records we found said the... Nathian (he'd almost said 'traitor') family on Marak was coded as *'The Head.'* Your name, Polly, contains the ancient word *'Poll'* which means *head*."

Polly looked at Stetson. "Is he always that sharp?"

"Every time," said Stetson.

"If you want to go into politics, Lewis," said Polly, "I'd be delighted to—"

"I'm already in politics as far as I want to be," growled Orne. "What I really want is to settle down with Di, catch up on some of the living I've missed."

Diana stiffened. "I never want to see, hear *from* or hear *of* Mr. Lewis Orne ever again!" she said. "That is final, emphatically final!"

Orne's shoulders drooped. He turned away, stumbled, and abruptly collapsed full length on the thick carpets. There was a collective gasp behind him.

Stetson barked: "Call a doctor! They warned me at the hospital he was still hanging on a thin thread!"

There was the sound of Polly's heavy footsteps running toward the hall.

"Lew!" It was Diana's voice. She dropped to her knees beside him, soft hands fumbling at his neck, his head.

"Turn him over and loosen his collar!" snapped Spencer. "Give him air!"

Gently, they turned Orne onto his back. He looked pale, Diana loosed his collar, buried her face against his neck. "Oh, Lew, I'm sorry," she sobbed. "I didn't mean it! Please, Lew...please don't die! Please!"

Orne opened his eyes, looked up at Spencer and Stetson. There was the sound of Polly's voice talking rapidly on the phone in the hall. He could feel Diana's cheek warm against his neck, the dampness of her tears. Slowly, deliberately, Orne winked at the two men.

ONE

TWENTY-SEVEN-YEAR-OLD Benjamin Bennett rolled over in his dormitory bed in the middle of the interstellar night thoroughly disgusted with himself. His Bombardier friends had often taunted him about his relationships with various members of the female population at Eos University. "One-Minute Bennett," they called him. No relationship he had ever seemed to last long enough to be memorable, let alone meaningful. Maybe they were right.

"It's not you," Ben told his date, throwing his left arm across his eyes, sunken in despair. "At least I don't *think* it's you. Ix! Who knows what it is?"

"Well, it's something," his date, Jeannie Borland, said.

Ms. Borland was a twenty-five-year-old, platinum blond graduate student in atmospheric chemistry whom Ben had met about a month earlier when Eos University had made its last planet-fall. He and his dorm mates—Eos dropouts called the Bombardiers—had gone kiting in the incredibly blue skies of Ala Tule 4 while the other students of the space-going university went about their various field trips down on the planet's surface. Ben had met Ms. Borland when he and the Bombardiers rested their wings in the AtChem gondola, lofting in the thermals of a placid mountain range. Ben thought he'd pursue her more aggressively when the university returned to its circuit through the known stars of the Sagittarius Alley.

And *this* was what happened.

Young men might reach their sexual peak at the age of nineteen or so, but it rarely tapered off so quickly. Moreover, Ben was in the best physical condition he had ever known. Though only five feet, ten inches tall, he was broad-shouldered and muscled enough to have won several wrestling scholarships when he was an undergraduate back on Earth. He worked out almost daily and theoretically *should* have been able to rise to the task.

In the semidarkness of the room, Jeannie Borland's illicit cigarette glowed dully. Her unaugmented breasts had that still-youthful pear shape to them, and her deliciously long legs should have inspired him to do *something*. But they didn't.

He sat up, sweeping his long black hair back into a ponytail, which he banded swiftly.

"Maybe it's the Ennui," Borland said, blowing a ghost of smoke to the ceiling.

"I think they put saltpeter in the food," Ben said.

Borland tapped an ash to the ashtray on Ben's nightstand. "Saltpeter? What's that?"

"Something they used to put in food to keep horny young boys from...getting frisky. Back in the old days."

"I don't believe it," Borland said. "That's barbaric. No one would do that here. Not on Eos."

"The Grays would," Ben remarked. "And they've got the Ainge behind them. After all, we can't have Mom and Dad worrying that Sally and Suzie will come home pregnant."

"No chance of that," Borland said listlessly, the tobacco calming her.

Ben eased out of bed, stepping into the gelatinous puddle his clothing made on the floor. Its response circuits activated at the familiar signature of his feet and his rugby jersey and shorts began flowing up his legs. When they found themselves back in their default configurations, they solidified. Ben's jersey said: RUGBY PLAYERS EAT THEIR DEAD. But only, Ben thought, if their testosterone levels were high. He moved his uncooperative "boys" around to help his underwear settle in.

"Look, this is the first time this has happened to me," Ben said. "You've got to believe me."

"Mmm," Borland said, tugging at her cigarette.

Actually, it had already happened—two weeks ago, with Christine Jensen, a biology student, and two days later, with Lisa Hold-away, an urban-dynamics sociology major who had been a student in one of the science classes he taught.

"It's the Ennui," Ms. Borland said with certainty.

She sat up and crushed out her cigarette. Sensing that the heat had gone out of the cigarette, the nightstand swallowed the ashtray. The room, meanwhile, quickly cleared the air.

Ben thought about the so-called Ennui, said to plague the spread of humanity across the stars. "That's a fairy tale. It's natural for civilization to slow down as it moves out among the stars. The Alley's a big place and we've only been traveling it for two hundred years."

"The pace of life in the Alley *has* slowed down," Borland said, stepping away from the bed. "They've got statistics and actuarial charts that prove it."

Ben refused to believe that the fabled Ennui was responsible for anything, let alone the apparent lack of technological advancements in the last two hundred years. It most certainly was *not* responsible for his temporary impotence. If, indeed, that's what it was.

Ms. Borland stepped into her clothing puddle and Ben watched as her panties and bra slithered to their default configurations. He swallowed hopelessly.

When humans left the confines of the Sol system, in 2098 C.E., to colonize nearby star systems, the sky seemed to be the proverbial limit for scientific advancements of all kinds. Peace had been secured on Earth; the Human Community formed. Faster-than-light technology was around the corner, and there was even the real possibility of medical science extending the life of the average human indefinitely. But sometime early in the twenty-third century, either just before or just after the En-

84

amorati appeared, technological and cultural advancements seemed to lose steam; there seemed to be fewer of them.

But then the Enamorati appeared, and savants everywhere forgot about the Ennui.

Humans had known that alien civilizations had existed since the early twenty-first century, when undecipherable signals came from a civilization in the Magellanic Clouds. These were quite accidental transmissions from a culture, now probably extinct, that was more than 200,000 light-years away. A few years later, a series of small, very intense gamma-ray explosions near Beta Lyra were picked up. Some were patterned, intense, and directional, as if weapons were being used. This was the so-called Beta Lyra Space War, but at 12,000 light-years the H.C. was a mere bystander. When the Enamorati arrived, humans suddenly found themselves involved in very real space travel with very real alien allies.

The Enamorati were a space-going culture from a world located 2,300 light-years toward the galactic center of the Milky Way Galaxy, deep inside the Sagittarius Alley. The Enamorati were missionaries from a culture whose planet had been destroyed in an unimaginable ecological disaster. The name "Enamorati" was the Italian equivalent of the attitude the aliens doctrinally shared toward all beings, sentient or otherwise, whom they happened to meet in their travels. The Enamorati had no interference clause, no Prime Directive that kept them out of planetary affairs not their own. Theirs was a mission of a religious bent, obliging them to offer the Human Community two things that it needed desperately: the location of habitable worlds *and* the transportation it took to get them there in a reasonable amount of time.

If the Enamorati had something like a Prime Directive, it came in the form of their staunch refusal to give humans the technical details of their giant Onesci Engines. The mathematics that led to the development of their FTL technology had been given to them ten thousand years ago by their greatest Avatar, a physicist named Onesci Lorii. Humans could use the Onesci Engines as freely as they wished, but they had to allow the Enamorati to handle the technology. This was a matter of deep seriousness for the Enamorati, and humans had to respect it if they wanted to ply the spaces between the stars.

Ben checked the time. "It isn't even fourteen hundred yet. Want to see what's going on in the student commons? Catch an Experience? They're showing *Mayberry Agonistes* tonight. Andy and Barney against the aliens?"

The romantic mood, however, had dissipated along with Ms. Borland's cigarette smoke.

"I don't think so, Ben," Jeannie Borland said, adjusting the chevrons of her collar. "Maybe some other time."

"They say it's the greatest science-fiction movie ever made," Ben said. "Wild Bill Kelso and George Reeves as Superman?"

"Sorry, Ben," Borland said.

At that moment, a gentle knocking came at the door to Ben's room.

"Are you expecting someone?" Borland asked, checking to see if her clothing had cohered properly.

For a moment Ben thought that his room's AI circuits had smelled Jeannie Borland's cigarettes and subsequently tattled to campus security. Tobacco was making a comeback on some of the worlds of the H.C., particularly among young people eager to leave their youth behind and to experience the world of mature grown-ups. Someone unaligned with the Grays—the university administration—or the Ainge religious faction on board the ship had apparently smuggled several different brands of cigarettes onto Eos a few planet stops ago and was now selling them to just about anyone who would buy them. They weren't quite illegal, but their use was definitely frowned upon.

"Not really," Ben said. "Stand back. Open," he then commanded the door.

"Oh!" Jeannie Borland said, gasping.

Standing in the doorway was an Enamorati. He stood there in his gray-green environment suit and had a sad expression on his face—routine for an Enamorati.

This Enamorati was different, however, for cradled in his frail, birdlike arms was the body of a little white polar bear.

"Please forgive me," the being said in slightly inflected English from inside his mist-filled helmet.

"I found your pet. It was right here before your door. I am so sorry."

This just wasn't Ben's day.

TWO

Eos University had a contingent of about a hundred Enamorati—all castes, their mates and progeny included. But beyond the often-seen Kuulo Kuumottoomaa—*kuulo* meant "steward" in their language—the other Enamorati usually remained in their chambers at the aft end of the four-thousand-foot-long ship, where they tended their enormous Engine. The lone Enamorati who stood before Ben's door, however, was not of the Kuulo caste. He was an Avatka, an engineer. And this engineer had a dead bear in his arms.

"It's not mine," Ben said to the Avatka. "I don't have a pet. Sorry."

The Avatka seemed puzzled, but there was no direct way to confirm this from the being's expressionless face. "Forgive me. I assumed that it was yours. It was lying before your door."

Ben looked off to his right. The hall was otherwise empty. "I don't think anyone on this floor has a pet. At least not a polar bear."

Jeannie Borland hovered behind Ben. "I've seen it before. It belongs to a girl in Cowden Hall."

"What's it doing here?" Ben asked.

Jeannie Borland shrugged.

Enamorati generally were no taller than five feet. But bolstered by their environment suits and with servomechanisms amplifying their shoulders and hips, they often seemed bigger than they actually were, and far more intimidating. The Enamorati were aware of this impression on human beings, and they often sought to avoid making it. This Enamorati seemed all too conscious of his sudden impact upon the young humans and tried to modulate his voice.

"I apologize for the disruption then. Could you help me return it to that person?" he asked of Ms. Borland.

She backed away. "I don't really know who owns it. Ben will help you though." She turned quickly to Ben. "Find me at the Museum Club at twenty-one hundred hours tonight, if. . . things change."

She edged past Ben, pulling a specter of tobacco behind her. She fairly raced to the nearest transit portal. A second later, she was gone.

The alien, oblivious to the nuances of human speech and social intercourse, hadn't a clue as to what had just passed between Ben and his erstwhile date. Instead, he gave the small animal to Ben. "If you could do this for me, I would be deeply in your debt," the alien said. "I do not wish to be of further discomfort."

Ben gently took the little bear from the alien's spindly arms, brushing the e-suit as he did. Ben thought he could detect a goblin of the air the Avatka breathed, but this, he knew, was impossible. A leak in the alien's e-suit would mean suffocation for the alien and severe nausea, perhaps even death, for any human nearby.

Though the little bear was definitely dead, there were no signs of blood on the animal's pelt. Moreover, no bones seemed crushed or broken. Strangulation did not seem the cause of the animal's passing, either.

For a fleeting moment Ben thought that the Avatka might have been responsible for killing the little bear, but that, too, seemed unlikely. The Enamorati claimed to have ended their species-wide violent stage about ten thousand years ago. They did not kill; they did not steal; they did not even lie. They lived entirely in the shadow of the religious vision of Onesci Lorii and had been doing so for thousands of years.

A yellowish mist swirled inside the alien's helmet. Pale and desiccated, the Enamorati looked like a race of mummified corpses with very sad eyes.

"Okay," Ben told the alien. "I'll do what I can."

"Thank you," the being said. "And should the animal's owner wish to speak with me about this, they may summon me at any time. I am the Avatka Viroo. Summon me directly or consult the *kuulo* first. I am at your disposal."

The frail being walked down the hallway, passing the transmission portal that Jeannie Borland had taken, and stepped into the connecting passageway. The being apparently wanted to walk back to the Enamorati compound rather than be teleported directly. Some Enamorati were odd that way.

Ben looked around. It was 2:00 P.M. on a Friday afternoon and most of Babbitt Hall was deserted—the students elsewhere in the ship. Most would be either in the field house or at the cinemas or in the Museum Club, starting their weekend early. The students who came from deeply religious Ainge families were probably still in their dorms studying. The polygamous Ainge, descendants from a splinter Mormon colony on the Isle of Ainge on Tau Ceti 4, still kept to clean, drug- and stimulant-free living. With any luck, Ben thought, the young woman who owned the bear would be a daughter of the Ainge and would be in her dorm studying with her suite mates before Friday-night services.

Ben stepped over to the wall. He pressed it with his hand and a luminescent menu for the ship's directory appeared. Any wall in any part of the ship had this feature. Ben tapped the wall menu command for FIND. But find who?

He tapped out the letters for the word PETS, then pressed ENTER. Pets were certainly allowed among the students, support staff, and faculty. But they were also registered with the university.

The word PETS appeared with a listing of two dozen kinds of animals as pets kept on board Eos University.

"A horse?" he said. "Someone has *horse* on the ship?" He would have to look up CYNTHIA JENEY later, just to satisfy his curiosity.

But someone did have a bear, so Ben pressed the glowing word

BEAR.

The name that appeared on the wall register read: JULIA WAXWING—COWDEN HALL—ROOM 220. Cowden Hall was the exclusively female dorm in Eos University and it was in the next wing over.

Ben toggled the com/pager at his belt and spoke into the pin at his collar. "ShipCom, open. Ben Bennett paging Julia Waxwing, please," he said. As he recalled, the nearby wing of Cowden Hall was filled with young women mostly studying the physical sciences. Whether Julia Waxwing was an undergraduate or a graduate, he didn't know and the wall menu didn't say.

The automated voice from ShipCom's computer said, *"Sorry. There is no response. There is no forward paging. Do you wish to leave a message?"*

"No," he said. "Com, close."

At that time of the afternoon, Julia Waxwing could be just about anywhere on the ship. University classes were never held on Fridays, but the labs were open, as was the library. Some professors even held office hours on Fridays.

On the other hand, the fact that there was no forward paging meant that regardless of where she was, Julia Waxwing didn't want to be disturbed.

"Now what?" he wondered aloud. He could just leave the bear in front of her dorm room, where she would find it whenever she got back from wherever she was. But that wouldn't do. Just because he'd had a dismal day didn't mean that he had to make it dismal for someone else.

But he *had* to do something.

To Ben's left, just a few yards away, the transit portal suddenly came alive with bluish light. Almost instantly, two figures fell from the portal's assembly ring and came crashing to the floor, sputtering with laughter.

These were friends of his, students he'd bonded with when they met at the beginning of the university's tour three years ago. One was George Clock, a gregarious ash-blond young man who used to be a geography major, specializing in satellite mapping techniques. The other boy was Jim Vees. Vees, a black American, had been an astronomy student until the Ennui—or something—got to him and he dropped out of his studies. He slept a lot, now. These were the Bombardiers. Only Tommy Rosales was missing at the moment.

Since George and Jim had bombed out of their programs, all they seemed to do was play as much as possible. Transit-hopping was one such form of recreation on the ship. Students often transit-hopped in an attempt to get high off the strange euphoric tingle that occurred when a person's molecules were stripped for transport over the ship's network of optical cables, then reassembled again. That's what these two had been doing. Hopping.

Ben stood above the two laughing Bombardiers with the dead bear in his arms. Clock pointed to the animal. "I'll bet this comes with a real *good* story," he said. He hadn't yet seen that the animal was lifeless.

"Believe it or not," Ben said, "an Avatka gave this to me a few moments ago. He found it right here, in front of my door."

"An Avatka? Here in Babbitt Hall?" Clock asked, climbing to his feet.

"Say, that animal looks dead," Jim Vees said. He was slower getting to his feet.

"It is dead," Ben said.

"Did the Avatka kill it?" Vees asked.

"I don't know," Ben said. "He said it was dead when he found it."

"Whose animal is it?" Vees asked, softly caressing its fur.

"It belongs to someone named Julia Waxwing, over in Cowden Hall. She's not answering her com and she's blocked all forward paging. Ever hear of her?"

The two dropouts shrugged and shook their heads.

Clock then said, "You know, she could be in the student commons, in the student media lounge with everybody else."

"Let's transit there," Vees said, always looking for an excuse to transit.

"What's going on at the commons?" Ben asked.

Vees smirked. "President Porter is going to release the contents of the last data bullet we snagged, the one we got right before we jumped into trans-space a couple of weeks ago."

"What's so important about that bullet?" Ben asked.

"Inside sources say that another ship exploded," Clock said. "A really big one this time. The bullet has all the information on it, but the administration's been debating whether to share the fully decompressed data with the rest of us. Maybe they think we'll riot if we get the whole story."

"What ship was it?" Ben asked.

"The *Annette Haven,* outward bound to Ross 154," Clock said. "At least that's the rumor. It's got the Grays worried."

Ben wasn't familiar with the *Annette Haven*. There were so many Engine-driven ships now in service that it was impossible to keep track of them all—freighters, people carriers, cargo vessels of all shapes and sizes, to say nothing of H.C. exploratory craft looking for new worlds to add to the Alley.

However, space travel had always been hazardous and ships every now and then still succumbed to systems failures, or even the unseen microparticle that would core a spaceship in a heartbeat. Disasters in space happened to humans and Enamorati alike.

"Someone at the student newspaper checked the H.C. manifest of ships in our data banks," Clock went on. "The *Haven* was a passenger liner. Big. It could transport at least nine hundred humans at a time. It had an Enamorati crew of twenty. If the Engine blew, there'd be nothing left but a transspace ripple."

95

Both the Ainge and the Enamorati happened to believe that trans-space was the actual body of God,
and that their duty was to lead pilgrims through
it. Most of the H.C. didn't see it that way, but used
the Engine-run ships anyway. Trans-space, however, did act like the Old Testament Jehovah and
saw fit to remind humans and Enamorati alike of
the dangers of space travel. Fiction had made space
travel seem effortless, even safe. But the truth was
that faster-than-light travel was just as hazardous
as slower-than-light travel, and many thousands of
lives had been lost in the last two and a half cen-
turies of space travel. Many more would be lost in
the future.

"How many Ainge Auditors were on the ship?" Ben
asked.

Clock laughed. "The *Haven* probably didn't have
more than one or two. It was just a liner."

"Darn the luck," Jim Vees said soberly, his transit
high having worn off. "Our Auditors should be so
lucky."

There was no love lost between Jim Vees and the
Ainge. Though Jim had come from Earth, part
of his family had converted to the Ainge religion
and had spent much of their efforts trying to get
the rest of the family to join. The Ainge, because
of their relationship to the Enamorati, represented
the fastest-growing religion in the *H.C.* But fifty
million followers of Ixion Smith were not enough
reason for Jim Vees to check his brain at the door.

"But get this," George Clock continued. "The student
newspaper says that one of our archaeology profes-

sors had a clone-son on the *Annette Haven*. Somebody famous, but they won't say who. Maybe Porter is going to tell us."

"An archaeology professor?" Ben asked.

"That's what they're saying," Clock affirmed.

Ben stepped back to the wall and called up the student directory once again. He came up with JULIA WAXWING, then asked for any kind of declared MAJOR.

On the screen appeared the word ARCHAEOLOGY.

"Figures," Ben said.

THREE

CONFIRMATION of the space death of the *Annette Haven* spread quickly through the halls of Eos University. There were no specifics. The data bullet had to travel light—the lighter, the faster. Undoubtedly, when Eos arrived at their next port of call, specifics regarding the passenger manifest and details of the cause of the ship's destruction would be much better known.

To Albert Holcombe, Regents Professor and chair of the archaeology department, the news was particularly devastating. As he had already shared with his colleagues, the clone of his second son, Joshua, a boy named Seth, had been on the *Annette Haven*.

Not that progeny mattered much to Albert Holcombe. The human race now numbered around ten billion, and a billion of those were clones, or the clones of clones. But Seth, at least as Holcombe remembered him, seemed to be the only Holcombe to have any life left in him, any *esprit, joie de vivre*. Even when Seth was a youngster on Tau Ceti 4, he would run circles around the fuddy-duddies of the Holcombe camp. It was no surprise to Holcombe when the boy became a StratoCaster, one of the BronzeAngel sky-runners, in fact. Holcombe always glowed with pride, thinking that a member of his family had pursued a disreputable career and actually made something of himself. But now the boy was dead—nothing more than blasted atoms in the indescribable vacuities of trans-space.

Unfortunately, Eos University was more than one hundred light-years from the Sol system at its farthest point on its four-year Alley tour. Holcombe didn't imagine that either Alex Cleddman—Eos's pilot—or any of the Grays would turn the university around just to accommodate his grief. In fact, the first thing that Captain Cleddman had announced at the hastily convened University Council meeting was that the ship would be continuing on its course to its next port of call. Holcombe merely nodded, accepting the grim ways of fate.

Cleddman, sometimes called the Cloudman by the students, was a stocky tree stump of a human being with massive arms, muscular legs, and no neck. He had played Australian-rules football in college, and the rough and tumble of the game had seemingly driven his head into his shoulders by several inches. He stood five feet five, compact and solid like a BennettCorp data bullet.

Cleddman placed a hand on Holcombe's shoulder, meaning to be sympathetic. "I never thought the *Haven* would go up. I've ridden her myself. I thought she was invincible."

"We all think we're invincible every now and then."

"I'll make sure you get the full report on the accident as soon as it's decompressed at the next port," the Cloudman said.

"I appreciate it," Holcombe said. "Thanks."

A junior member of the mathematics department in the back of the Council hall stood up and looked around. "Excuse me, Captain. Shouldn't one of the Auditors be present at this meeting? It's written in the faculty bylaws. It's part of our charter."

"I notified them," Cleddman said, turning. "But they're preparing for Friday-night services."

"Then perhaps we can wait until tomorrow or Monday," said the faculty member. Like the Ainge priests and the university administration personnel, this young man wore a gray tunic. Holcombe despised gray...

Captain Cleddman cut off the faculty member with a slight gesture. "I understand your concern, Dr. DeGroot, but we are letting the Kuulo stand in for High Auditor Nethercott. Will you allow that?"

Off to the left of the podium stood a hologram projection stage. A 3D image hovered there, that of the ranking Enamorati, the Kuulo Kuumottoomaa. The Kuulo was actually somewhere deep inside the Enamorati compound at the far end of the giant ship.

It was easier for him to be present this way and to speak without being locked in his e-suit.

The alien looked in the direction of Dr. DeGroot. His Standard English was flawless as he spoke. "I will advise Mr. Nethercott on the content of the meeting as soon as he is available. Our Ainge brothers will be fully informed."

"That's acceptable," Dr. DeGroot said.

Holcombe thought he could detect a note of disappointment in DeGroot's acquiescence. Everybody knew there were factions on the ship that were itching to catch their pilot, who was not of the Ainge religion, in a lapse of protocol. But Cleddman would never give them the chance. Hooray for Cleddman.

The alien's next words, surprisingly, were for him. "Albert Holcombe, we, too, share your loss. Many of our own perished on the HCSV *Annette Haven*. The loss is no less meaningful to us. I can assure you that our engineers will do what they can to make certain that a similar accident doesn't happen to us."

The pilot cleared his throat. "That's why I called this meeting. This is as good a time as any to bring the matter up, but in light of what's just happened to the *Haven,* I think it's time we took up the proposal Physics and Mechanical Engineering made last year when the *Aurora Lee* was lost in transit to Beta Draconis 5."

The Council hall fell absolutely silent. Even Holcombe hadn't expected something like this.

"No offense, Kuulo," the Cloudman said, "but humans feel better if they're working on their own problems instead of waiting around for someone else to deal with them."

"What are you saying, Mr. Cleddman?" someone asked in the rear.

"Physics and Engineering have three different star-drive systems in development that could rival the capacities of an Onesci Engine. The math is there and I've seen the schematics. I think we should consider shifting all of our technical resources over to Physics and Engineering to see if we can get one of the stardrive systems up and running. For real."

The forty-member Council started rumbling and shifting about in their seats. Holcombe noticed that the 3D image of the Kuulo Kuumottoomaa remained impassive.

"You're thinking about going your own way, aren't you," someone else said.

"*Our* way," the Cloudman responded. "I have made it clear many, many times that I don't like my fate being in the hands of. . . others. Sorry, Kuulo. This is the best opportunity humankind has had in two hundred years. We've got to try sometime. I think now is the time."

Dr. DeGroot stood up once again. "I can see why you didn't want the Ainge here, Mr. Cleddman," he said heatedly. "Without the Engines, the Ainge would have no authority on a human vessel, now, would they?"

"Dr. DeGroot, this isn't about the Ainge," Cleddman said firmly. "This is about powering our own vessels with our own engines, doing our own technical checks to see that all systems are working the way they should be working—and if they *do* blow up in trans-space, then we can examine the engines themselves, if anything's left, to see for ourselves what went wrong."

Holcombe though he could hear a page of history turning over a massive leaf. Cleddman had suggested nothing less than an act of absolute liberation, an act many human beings—billions of them, in fact—might not want. Those people, members of the vast Ainge Church, would have the most to lose, at least in terms of political influence.

The Enamorati Compact was signed on Tau Ceti 4 in 2205 C.E. by Ixion Smith, president of the Ainge, acting on behalf of the Human Community. It formally bound humans to respect the religious aspects of the Onesci Engines. No ship using Onesci Engines could engage in war; acts of piracy or unprovoked violence were forbidden. But along with the Enamorati engineers, several humans, high priests of the Ainge religion called Auditors, would always accompany the Enamorati. Their relationship to the Enamorati was special and inviolate. Cleddman had just suggested an end to all that.

Humans *did* have a form of trans-light travel, but it was limited, employing molecular compression based on nearly ancient fractal mathematics. So-called bullets of compressed matter, the biggest a millimeter in diameter, could be shot through trans-space to allow for a decent system of real-time communications between worlds light-years apart. The mysteries of trans-space, let alone Engines efficient enough to move people through it, still eluded the best minds of the Human Community.

The Kuulo Kuumottoomaa held up his hand, pleading. "Mr. Cleddman, we believe that our Engines are the best that can be made, especially for a ship this size. And I hope you understand that we have no desire to die in space, either. When we know more of what happened to the *Annette Haven,* we will do everything we can to make certain this great ship will not suffer the same fate."

"I'm sure you will," Cleddman said. "But I would much rather have a greater say over how I live and die than I have now. If the problem *is* with the Engines, then I want to know exactly why. But you're never going to share that information with us, and that we can no longer tolerate."

"Speak for yourself, Alex," said Dr. DeGroot.

"I'm speaking for myself and every human being who has died in-transit in the last hundred years. I'm also speaking for you, too. I'm an equal-opportunity pilot. I fly anybody. I just want to arrive in one piece."

"The odds of perishing in-transit are still ten million to one," Dr. DeGroot said. "And I trust the Enamorati *and* their Engines."

A female faculty member from Biochemistry stood up. "Captain, you can't possibly do this without the approval of the university administration and faculty. We're a university first, a spaceship second."

"The Eos University charter allows me to take control of the ship if or when the *vessel* is threatened. I'm not invoking that charter now. But, I *will* if I have to. And if I have to, I want to be ready. This shouldn't disturb the functions of the university. And, yes, I will consult the administration if or when the time comes for us to break away."

"Are we close?" a voice asked from the rear.

"Not yet," Cleddman admitted.

"Then isn't this a little hasty?" someone else asked. "We don't know what happened to the *Annette Haven*. It may have had nothing to do with its Engine."

"This has been brewing for quite some time now," Cleddman told them. "I'm not the only pilot in the H.C. who feels this way.

But as far as I know, we're the only ones in a position to test the advances we've made so far. And, I might add, if we pull this off, Eos University will be unsurpassed in excellence and fame."

"You're doing this because you don't like the Enamorati," Professor DeGroot said.

"No, I'm doing this because I don't like to be blown up," Cleddman said. "And I don't think you do, either. In any event, when the time comes I will run this through all the proper channels and nobody on the Council will be left out of the debate. But as I said earlier, it's my job to maintain our safety. This is definitely *not* a political matter."

"Not yet, it isn't," grumbled Professor DeGroot.

104

With that, the 3D image of the Kuulo winked out. Evidently, the Kuulo had heard all he wanted to hear; so had a number of others.

The impromptu meeting seemed to be at an end.

Buy the book to read the rest of this great adventure

Search for 9781604501902 (book's ISBN) at your favorite online bookstore, order through your favorite neighbourhood store

or

visit
www.PhoenixPick.com
for easy links to purchasing options from major retailers.

MORE TITLES FROM PHOENIX PICK

Poul Anderson
Security
The Burning Bridge

Paul Cook
The Engines of Dawn
Fortress on the Sun

Andre Norton
Voodoo Planet
Key Out of Time

John Campbell
The Ultimate Weapon

Visit

www.PhoenixPick.com

to buy these and many other great sci-fi/fantasy titles

www.ingramcontent.com/pod-product-compliance
Lightning Source LLC
Chambersburg PA
CBHW020620130626
46552CB00003B/1057